READING CORNER

PHONICS

Mum's Red Hat

Written by
Margaret Nash

Illustrated by
Jan Smith

Practising CVC words with
short vowel sounds + and / the / to

First published in 2009 by
Franklin Watts
338 Euston Road
London NW1 3BH

Franklin Watts Australia
Hachette Children's Books
Level 17/207 Kent Street
Sydney NSW 2000

Text © Margaret Nash 2009
Illustration © Jan Smith 2009

A CIP catalogue record for this book is available
from the British Library.

ISBN: 978 0 7496 9147 9 (hbk)
ISBN: 978 0 7496 9156 1 (pbk)

Series Editor: Jackie Hamley
Series Advisors: Dr Barrie Wade, Dr Hilary Minns
Series Designer: Jonathan Hair

Printed in China

Franklin Watts is a division of
Hachette Children's Books,
an Hachette UK company
www.hachette.co.uk

There is a puzzle at the end of this book.
Here are the answers for you to check later!

The matching words are:
Sid   did, hid, lid
hat   cat, mat, rat
Mum   gum, hum, sum
bin   din, pin, tin

Mum put on a big red hat.

3

But Sid the dog got it.

5

"Bad dog, Sid!"

Sid ran in the mud.

9

He ran to the tip.

10

11

"Bad dog, Sid!"

13

Sid got in the bin.

15

Mum got the hat.

17

But the hat is not red.

18

19

And bad dog Sid is in his bed!

21

Puzzle Time!

Match the words that rhyme to the pictures!

Sid

hum

pin

cat

mat

hat

did

tin

Mum

hid

din

gum

rat

sum

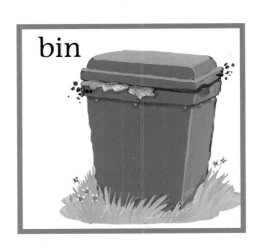

bin

lid

See page 2 for answers!

Notes for parents and teachers

READING CORNER PHONICS has been structured to provide maximum support for children learning to read through synthetic phonics. The stories are designed for independent reading but may also be used by adults for sharing with young children.

The teaching of early reading through synthetic phonics focuses on the 44 sounds in the English language, and how these sounds correspond to their written form in the 26 letters of the alphabet. Carefully controlled vocabulary makes these books accessible for children at different stages of phonics teaching, progressing from simple CVC (consonant-vowel-consonant) words such as "top" (t-o-p) to trisyllabic words such as "messenger" (mess-en-ger). READING CORNER PHONICS allows children to read words in context, and also provides visual clues and repetition to further support their reading. These books will help develop the all important confidence in the new reader, and encourage a love of reading that will last a lifetime!

If you are reading this book with a child, here are a few tips:

1. Talk about the story before you start reading. Look at the cover and the title. What might the story be about? Why might the child like it?

2. Encourage the child to reread the story, and to retell the story in their own words, using the illustrations to remind them what has happened.

3. Discuss the story and see if the child can relate it to their own experience, or perhaps compare it to another story they know.

4. Give praise! Small mistakes need not always be corrected. If a child is stuck on a word, ask them to try and sound it out and then blend it together again, or model this yourself. For example "wish" w-i-sh "wish".

READING CORNER PHONICS covers two grades of synthetic phonics teaching, with three levels at each grade. Each level has a certain number of words per story, indicated by the number of bars on the spine of the book:

GRADE 1	
50 words	CVC words with short vowel sounds
70 words	CVC words plus sounds of more than one letter
100 words	Sounds of more than one letter, simple polysyllabic words

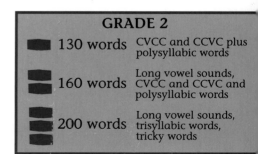

GRADE 2	
130 words	CVCC and CCVC plus polysyllabic words
160 words	Long vowel sounds, CVCC and CCVC and polysyllabic words
200 words	Long vowel sounds, trisyllabic words, tricky words